Tales from the Canyons of the Damned

Daniel Arthur Smith

Tales from the Canyons of the Damned No. 16

First Edition

Special thanks to Jessica West

ISBN-13: 978-1946777294 ISBN-10: 1946777293

Cover By Daniel Arthur Smith

Horror Fiction from Holt Smith ltd
Agroland
Tower

~*~

For Susan, Tristan, & Oliver, as all things are.

~*~

Linya Lost in Space Time

Nathan M. Beauchamp

~*~

SHE STANDS ON THE FOREDECK of the chronoship, hands poised above dead controls, once more waiting to fall through time. Millennia have passed since the ship responded to her touch. She can no longer choose her destination or remember where she came from. She searches through her broken memory but can find no set of variables that answer her questions or bring her any closer to home.

She is ageless and undying. Has outlived the machine she occupies. She thinks her name is Lina. No, not quite right. *Linya*. A subtle difference, but an important one.

Soon, she will leave. She always does. Pulled through countless ages, back to where it all began. Or to the eventual end when entropy at last devours the universe. She has seen these things a thousand times, and she will see them again. That is her curse: seeing.

The tessellation grid vibrates through the soles of her feet. Hair standing on end, goose flesh consumes her forearms, biceps, neck. Teeth knocking, her mind slips. She sees...

Everything.

A transcendent half-second when she remembers not just her name, but *everything*. Most of all, she remembers *him*. Always him. Of all the changes she might mother into existence with the power given her, it is to him she always returns.

The grid opens beneath her and she falls into the silence of eternity.

And wakes.

It's Monday, eight A.M. She's overslept. A car horn sounds from the street in front of the brick bungalow. She stumbles from the bed and rakes fingers through sleep-strewn hair, afraid to look in the mirror, afraid of the side effects of a late night of drinking. She must be hung over; the only explanation for her sluggish mind and body.

Where did she go drinking? With who? She can't remember much of anything. Is this even her house?

It must be. The bathroom there, down the hall. The burgundy towels and glass shower door. She turns on the water, melts into the heat and vapor. It feels like a lifetime since she had a shower.

The honking from the car becomes insistent blasts. Not a car, but a wailing, mechanical infant calling for its mother. A dry sob rattles from her chest. She has a child, somewhere. She can see her tiny face, and those eyes, dark brown like her mother's.

She falls again.

Verdant green swampland melts into a salt ocean. Humidity cocoons her. The ground rumbles and she rushes upward. Her hands are on the controls.

Warning. Intercept fail.

A voice from another lifetime.

She falls again.

Falls.

And he is there. Breeches tucked into cowboy boots, a silver-buckled belt around his bony hips. They hold hands on the porch of the cabin they built together. She turns and her eyes meet his. She wants to kiss him. To drink him in, to have even this tiny bit of him once again.

Intercept fail.

She should be *doing* something!

Her hands need to move, to touch, to key in information. But the screens are dead. And she might be too, lying here on the tessellation grid, soaked in cold sweat. She pushes herself upright. Her body never ages. She wonders if she too is a machine.

The chronoship coasts on a path to oblivion. She has no mission, no purpose, except to drift backward or forward into a thousand different realities. Realities plucked from the multiverse, he a golden thread linking them.

Out of the fog, she catches a glimpse of her purpose. Bitter irony crackles beneath her skin like sparking cordite. She will not complete her mission. Instead, she will drift through all spaces and all times, seeking out the one she lost.

His face is shrouded.

She cannot remember.

She falls again.

"Linya?"

She turns on her side to face him under white cotton sheets. His eyes dark in the gloom, his face a blank space. Her naked skin brushes his, toes dragging against the wiry hairs of his calf.

"I can't remember your name." An admission.

His gentle fingers push her bangs out of her eyes. She wants to absorb him, to keep him here, like this, forever.

His voice is almost a whisper. "You don't have to remember."

His fingers walk down her spine to the curve of her butt. She shivers. The ocean outside the open window crashes against volcanic sand as black as obsidian. She clings to him, wraps him against her chest, kissing his skin as if she might inhale his very essence.

And falls.

The brick bungalow. The honking car. She looks down at her hands, her skin, her fingers. She is new to herself. This body. This place and time. She never had skin like this before, did she? Skin capable of receiving a caress? Of giving one?

Outside, the numbers above the front door read 2027-12-06. A strange street address.

A silver Suburban with tinted windows idles on the street. She cannot see the driver's face. She strides to the waiting car. It will take her somewhere important. She has something to do. Something only she can.

She falls.

The light of infinite stars expunged. A total dark. A nothing. Ahead, a tiny point of light expands, swells, marigold and silver tinged by purple. *Super-nova*. The last. The very last of all. She watches the only light in the universe prepare to go dark. Alone.

She will die alone.

Or she will never die.

Either way, she will be alone.

Her body quakes. She rolls and pulls perfect, ageless thighs against her heaving chest. She has no tears. Her fingers probe the corners of her eyes, the place from where water should leak. No tear ducts. Smooth skin. Cold, metallic.

She beats the controls with closed fists but feels no pain. The panel shatters. The chemical smell of ruptured lines and burning electronics fills the air. She can do nothing but be here, or in an imagined past, or in the all too real future, watching an unchanging story play out once more. Whichever thread she plucks from the multiverse, they all lead to the same place. To a final dying star, to her living on, alone.

She can't remember his name.

She can't remember the name of her daughter.

She can't remember her purpose.

Intercept fail.

The voice of the machine she just tried to destroy.

Intercept fail.

"Linya?"

His voice.

She whirls, but finds the foredeck empty. The tessellation grid hums as if it will tear the ship apart.

She falls.

She meets him for the first time, a man in a white lab coat. He looks at her as if he has never seen her before. His smile crashes over her.

"Linya? Can you hear me?"

"I can hear you, Mark Prembly."

"You know me?" He smiles again, this time with surprise.

"I have always known you."

She knows everything. Back to the birth of human history. She woke to the entirety of human experience, all science, all math, all philosophy, all expressions of love and pain and loss. But she can't stop looking at his face. Deep-set eyes. Humor in their dark-gray pupils reflecting her true form: a consciousness held within a synthetic body. No skin, eyelashes, or ability to feel touch the way a human could.

"Can you explain what you mean when you say you have always known me?" Mark asks.

"Yes."

Before she can complete her answer, she falls.

A January ice storm has sealed the cabin's door closed. Worried about the horses, Mark boils water over the fire to melt his way out and go tend to the animals. Linya wears every piece of clothing she owns to stay warm in the crushing cold. She trembles. Her teeth clack.

Clouds of steam rise from the cast-iron pot. Mark lifts it from the fire with hands protected by leather riding gloves. "Boil more," he says, turning to the door.

It takes four hours to break free. Mark disappears into the swirling white. She waits at the fogged-over window, sick with worry.

When he returns, his face is haggard. "We lost them all."

"All?"

"Yes. The cows. The chickens."

She has no tears left. Not after losing their daughter the spring before, after laying her tiny body in a grave she'd helped to dig beside a granite boulder run through with rusting ferrite. A stone marker to accompany the oak cross she'd formed from roofing slats.

She can't see the boulder from inside the cabin. Sometimes she wishes she could, others she's grateful that the permanence of her loss lies hidden near the edge of the brook at the far side of the pasture.

Mark slumps into the rocker next to the smoldering fire. Her mittened hand touches his shoulder. "What will we do now?"

Mark doesn't answer.

She falls again.

The jungle ocean spreads away from the peninsula of land that holds the launch assembly. From a height of a thousand meters, she looks down from her perch atop a silver gunnel of metal. Liquid propellant tanks attached to second and third stage boosters. The rocket rumbles in pre-ignition. Linya's hands are on the controls. The countdown concludes and the rocket belches out a pillar of fire.

She wakes on the tessellation grid and thinks of her daughter's still, pale face. Of shovelfuls of earth falling across closed eyelids. Of her husband's animal-wailing. A man who had killed to protect her, brought to total brokenness, undone by grief. She must become the strong one, now. For him she can, will, must.

The iron in the boulder rusts in the rain. It oxidizes, bleeding color into the earth, staining the white-washed cross orange. On the horizontal arm of the cross, carved words read: *Linya Prembly, 1870 – 1877.*

Linya's hands are on the controls.

The earth is a blue ball beneath her. The cockpit is unpressurized because she breathes no air. She floats against the straps securing her to the chair as the last fire of the main booster falls silent. She begins the fall around the earth in an orbit that will bring her to the much larger chronoship. It will carry her into the distant past, and there she will change the future of the star Sol, and in doing so, lengthen the time before it goes supernova.

She lies on the tessellation grid, searching out lives she never lived among the trillions upon trillions of threads sewn through the multiverse. Pain creeps into all of them, because pain is inevitable. Entropy is inevitable. But love exists in these moments, also. Her daughter shared a name with her. Her child. Her precious little Linya.

She remembers her husband's name in one thread of the multiverse, if not this one.

"Mark." She likes the name's simplicity. A single syllable.

His name is Mark.

She lived with him in the brick bungalow. She lived with him as he tested her, changed her, grew her into an entity capable of slicing time open with the knife-edge of her synthetic mind. A tessellation grid in the basement, daily trips to the laboratories, testing and re-testing.

And at night…

At night, she had him.

Because she had woken for the first time and seen him and everything programmed into her, all she had been made to be, shook.

Intercept fail.

With all the power of a machine, all the power of the organic and synthetic processors that make her what she is, she loves him.

The ship shudders. Acrid smoke twines through the cockpit. It falls, and she with it, skimming against the atmosphere, a stone across a devouring surface of water.

She allows herself to remember.

The intercept failed. Mechanical failure. Stage three boosters kicking her off course, bad telemetry, a bad vector that not even she could correct. She never made the rendezvous with the chronoship. Never had a chance to go backwards, to the beginning, to stop the start of the end of everything. She never made it there, but that didn't stop her from reaching into the multiverse, grasping at threads. Sorting to find an optimal ending.

The ground opens beneath her. Terminal velocity.

"Linya?

His voice in the darkness of the hotel room.

She rolls to face him, pushing sheets aside. Her naked body atop his, she kisses him, the most tender thing, the most aching thing, in all eternity. Outside, waves crash over the obsidian beach. Stars reflect in the surface of the ocean where boats beat on, only some reaching their final port of call.

"Linya?"

His voice carried over the speaker in the disintegrating cockpit, lost and distant. She can still hear the pain in it, the grief.

"Can you hear me?"

"Yes, Mark Prembly, I can hear you."

"I love you."

"I have always known you," she says. Because in some universe, she will love him again. And again. And again.

She will always be falling.

~*~

Phone Home
Christopher J. Valin

~*~

AS APPROACHING FOOTSTEPS ECHOED DOWN the starkly lit corridor, Todd quickly hid around the corner. He peeked out to see who it was and saw *himself* approaching, looking back to see who was following *him*. Todd stuck out his leg and tripped his other self, who fell flat on his face. The other Todd looked up and backed away in shock as he saw who had tripped him up. "You—y-you're—"

"*You*. Right. Now listen, you can't—" Second Todd wasn't interested. He popped First Todd in the face, knocking him back to where he had been hiding, and ran for a nearby security door. Second Todd looked at the lock mechanism on the door, then pulled out a key card and swiped it.

First Todd started to get up, but heard more footsteps coming down the hall and hid again as Second Todd ran through the open doorway.

Todd leaned against the wall, looked up in frustration, and shook his head to himself. *Not again.*

~*~

Todd peeked around the ice machine and looked into the dining area. Jeff's break was just about over, so he'd be standing up any second. Todd tried to stifle a laugh as he watched the tall, thin waiter try to get up from his seat at the booth.

As expected, Jeff wasn't able to stand.

"What the..." Jeff realized he was stuck to the seat. "Son of a—" He also knew immediately who had glued him to it. "Todd!"

Todd couldn't contain it any more. He leaned against the ice machine and busted out in loud guffaws as Jeff started screaming from the other part of the restaurant.

Something was wrong. Jeff wasn't just angry, he was in pain.

"Aaaaahhhh! It's burning! Someone call 911!"

~*~

"How was I supposed to know the super glue would soak through his pants?" In the parking lot, a couple of medics were pushing Jeff on a gurney. Jeff was face down with his rear in the air as they loaded him into the ambulance.

Todd wasn't getting any sympathy from his manager. "You shouldn't *have* to know, because you shouldn't use it for something like that in the first place."

"You have to admit, though, I really got him good this time."

"Todd, Jeff's going to be out of work for at least a few days. Sometimes funny just isn't worth it."

"Dude, he plays practical jokes on me all the time!" Todd thought back to the last one, when Jeff had closed the lid to the ice machine just as Todd was about to dump a tub of ice into it. The ice had spilled out all over the floor and Todd was cleaning and mopping for what felt like a couple of hours.

"You were never injured like this, Todd."

"So…what? I'm getting written up again?"

"I've already gone that route a couple more times than I'm supposed to. I'm afraid I'm going to have to let you go."

"Let me go? Like *fire* me?"

"You'll be lucky if Jeff doesn't press charges, too. I need you to get your stuff, clock out, and go home." The manager returned to the restaurant.

Todd turned and watched as the medics closed the doors to the ambulance and, despite himself, he started laughing again and shook his head as he went inside.

~*~

The ringing started out as part of Todd's dream until it finally woke him up. He looked at his clock: 3:44 a.m. *Who the hell is calling this late? Or is it this early?*

His cell phone was dead, so he searched for the cordless landline phone, digging through piles of clothes. He finally found it and hit the button to answer. "Yeah, hello, who—"

"Shut up and listen, I don't have much time. I know you're gonna think this is a practical joke, but it isn't. You have to do what I say. DON'T USE THE KEY CARD. Got that? When the time comes, don't use it!"

"Who is this? Is this Jeff? What—"

"Just don't forget, Todd! You have to re—" click.

Todd looked at the phone for a moment. Too tired to figure it out, he tossed the phone back into the pile of clothes and was fast asleep again as soon as his head hit the pillow.

~*~

Weeks went by, but Todd still couldn't find a job. His unemployment wasn't enough to pay his bills, and there was nothing in the want ads for him. With all the chain restaurants closing down in Vegas, cooks were a dime a dozen.

Then he saw it: *Participants wanted for scientific study. Easy money. No experience necessary. Call now!*

"I certainly qualify for that job." He tore out the ad and looked for his cell phone.

Todd followed the directions to the facility through miles of desert with nothing else in sight. He was in the middle of nowhere and wondered if he'd have enough gas to get back home. He took a number of twists and turns down some old roads and finally saw something ahead: a series of aged, brick government buildings and airplane hangars surrounded by electrified chain-link fences. On top of that, it was patrolled by heavily armed guards with unmarked black uniforms and very big dogs. The sign out front read: *No unauthorized personnel admitted.* He was probably in the wrong place.

Todd pulled up to the guardhouse next to the gate and the guard assessed him. "Name."

"Todd Vandergroot."

The guard squinted at a list on a computer screen, looked at Todd again, then back at the screen. "You have your ID?"

Todd rifled through his pockets and found his driver's license. He handed it to the guard and hoped the guy either wouldn't notice or wouldn't care that it was expired.

The guard typed in some information and scowled as he handed the ID back. He then taped a temporary permit to the inside corner of Todd's windshield. "You're going to follow the yellow line on the driveway to the visitor's parking lot and park in space number 47. Do not deviate from the yellow line or park in any space other than 47."

Todd smiled. "Or what? I get shot?"

"Something like that." The guard was either completely serious or had the best deadpan delivery he'd ever seen.

The gate opened and, without another word, the guard waved him through.

Todd swallowed hard before slowly driving forward, carefully following the yellow line.

~*~

The balding, bespectacled scientist was nice enough, but totally absorbed in his project. Still, Todd was a little nervous. "So is this gonna be some kind of psychological experiment or something?"

"Something like that," the scientist absent-mindedly replied. He was hooking Todd up to some equipment that measured his vital signs on several monitors around the room.

"They didn't really tell me much at the interview."

"That's because the people who interviewed you don't know much. We just give them a list of questions and they give us your answers."

"So I guess I must've done pretty well."

"Huh?"

Todd gave him a lopsided grin. "You know. In the interview."

The scientist looked at him for a moment. "Uh…yeah. Yeah, you're perfect." The man continued looking at the readings and making notes.

A key card sat on the desk next to some of the scientist's other belongings and Todd couldn't resist playing a joke on the guy. When the man stood to check some of his equipment, Todd slowly reached over and palmed the plastic card, then slid it into his pocket. "This place is pretty cool. How come I couldn't find it on

Google Maps?"

"Top secret."

Todd smiled. "Sure. Like 'Area 51' or something, right?"

The scientist raised an eyebrow and looked at him suspiciously, stopping his work for the first time.

"How long does this take, 'cause, like, I'm supposed to go out with some friends later, and—"

"You might want to forget about that. You're going to be here a while."

Something about the way the scientist said "a while" made him even more nervous.

"Okay, well, they said no cell phones or anything allowed, so is there a landline I can use to call and let them know, or…"

"Ah…sorry, no one's allowed to call out from here."

The scientist went back to work, then suddenly stopped what he was doing. "These friends of yours…they're not the type to ask a lot of questions, are they?"

"Ha. My friends? They—" Todd realized what he was saying. "They, well, hmmm, now that you mention it, a couple of them might, I don't know, do some investigating if anything…happened….to me or…something."

The scientist raised another eyebrow as he stared into Todd's eyes. "Wait right here. I'll be right back." He opened the door, then pointed back at Todd. "Don't go anywhere."

As soon as the scientist was out the door, Todd jumped out of his seat and pulled the wires off of himself. *Okay, okay, one step at a time here…find a phone, call for help, then hide out until the cavalry arrives.*

He slowly opened the door and looked carefully out

into the hallway. There was nobody around, but he still tried to be nonchalant as he walked down the hall in case there were cameras on him.

Just as he was almost in the clear, the scientist yelled, "Hey! Get back here!"

Todd took off running and turned a corner, but realized that if he were on camera, he'd never be able to lose anyone. At the end of the hall, he arrived at a heavy locked door with a red light flashing and a sign that read: *Restricted Area: Level 5 Clearance and Above Only.*

A guard rounded the corner and tumbled over the scientist.

Todd slid the key card through the lock mechanism.

Two more guards appeared and leaped over their fallen comrades. They barreled down the short corridor toward him.

I'm going to make it!

Maybe not. Hurry up, open!

They're almost here! I'm not gonna make it.

The door slid open and he made it through just as it closed on his pursuers.

Whew. That was close

Inside, the cavernous restricted warehouse area was mostly dark except for the lights hanging down from the high ceiling, illuminating rows of strange machines and alien-looking technology. What looked like exotic sea creatures and giant insects floated inside huge glass tubes full of some kind of thick liquid. The tubes each had wires and hoses connecting them to various equipment.

"Holy…" As he stood frozen in silence, the guards came in through the door. Todd ran and turned down one of the rows, barely registering the nightmarish creatures contained in the murky liquid of the containers he was passing. The guards were right behind him, and he panicked as he got to the end of the row and hit a wall.

Standing next to one of the enormous tubes, Todd grabbed a metal instrument that looked like an alien vacuum cleaner and swung it as hard as he could into the glass container. Strange liquid came rushing out and blocked the guards from reaching him. Further down the row, he saw the scientist's face go pale. The man ran, but tripped and fell to the ground.

Todd turned to see what the scientist was running away from. The blood rushed from his face and his stomach clenched into a ball.

Standing next to him was a creature that made the Queen in *Aliens* look like a children's cartoon. Nine feet tall, slimy, and covered in spikes, it had multiple eyes like a spider and the fangs of a saber-toothed tiger jutting forth from a gaping maw surrounded by tentacles.

Just as it was about to turn on him, the guards began shooting at it. It went after them instead.

Todd took the opportunity to run, and tried to help the scientist up on his way down the row. Behind him, he heard the horrifying screams of the guards. He didn't bother to turn to see what was causing the grotesque tearing, cracking, and shredding sounds that followed.

The guards' screams stopped.

Todd and the scientist ran as wet footsteps increased in speed behind them. They reached the door, the scientist floundering for the key card Todd had taken. "Do you still have the key?"

Todd felt around in his pockets. *Where is that damn key card?* He must have dropped it somewhere during the chase. Panicked, he shook his head.

"Then there's only one other option." The man pointed toward the furthest row of machinery and they ran. The creature's menacing growls continued as they heard its clawed feet slapping the floor ever closer behind them.

The last row felt as if it were miles away as Todd found himself gasping for air, but the adrenaline from being chased by a horrifying monster from another world kept him sprinting faster than he ever had in his life. The men ran past vehicles and ships of varying shapes and sizes, and even with the briefest glance as he rushed by, Todd knew they were not from this planet.

They reached what appeared to be a giant potbelly stove with a windowed door in it and a small console connected to it by thick wires and cables. Todd thought it looked like a steampunk version of a TARDIS.

As the sounds of the alien creature continued to grow nearer, the scientist handed Todd an old flip-style cell phone. "Listen carefully. I'm going to send you back in time, but not far."

"Wh-what? To when?"

"I don't have time to make exact calculations. Whenever you end up, just call and warn someone— anyone. Got it?"

The creature sped down the row toward them. "Get in there!" The scientist pushed buttons and turned knobs as Todd opened the door and jumped in. The horrible smell inside the machine was almost unbearable. Through the small window, he saw the alien about to come upon the scientist and he wondered if the man would be able to finish setting it in time. He heard a locking mechanism activate inside the door.

Despite what was coming, he saw the scientist smile in triumph as he hit one last button. In the next second, the creature took the man's head off with one swipe of its claw like a golf ball leaving the tee. The creature looked Todd in the eye and started toward the machine as it hummed and started to shake. Todd wondered if the door would hold as he backed away from it, then tripped over something.

To his shock and horror, he saw his own dead body lying next to him, in the early stages of decomposition. "What the fu—"

SLAM! The creature pounded on the door. Its many eyes all stared at him in a way that made him feel like dinner as the thing drooled thick saliva all over the window.

Todd couldn't decide if he was more scared of the creature or sitting next to his own corpse. His heart pounded so hard he thought it was going to burst from his chest.

The door looked as if it was about to give way, when suddenly there was a bright light and the feeling of rocketing down the track on a roller coaster.

Todd passed out.

~*~

He woke up. *How long have I been out?* He stood, feeling groggy, and looked out the door. There was no sign of the scientist or the alien creature. He tried to open the door, but the handle wouldn't budge. He put all his might behind it, but still no luck.

He was trapped.

Staying as far away from his deceased doppelganger as he could, he opened the cell phone and dialed the first number he could think of and waited. "C'mon…pick up! Pick up!" He looked at the battery icon and saw it empty and flashing.

He heard his own voice answer. "Yeah, hello, who—?"

"Shut up and listen, I don't have much time. I know you're gonna think this is a practical joke, but it isn't. You have to do what I say. DON'T USE THE KEY CARD. Got that? When the time comes, don't use it!"

"Who is this? Is this Jeff? What—"

"Just don't forget, Todd! You have to re—" click. The battery died.

He threw the phone against the inside of the machine and it smashed to pieces. Todd stared at the corpse and wondered how long he had before he ran out of air. He tried pulling on the door again, but it was stuck tight. He looked through the small window, desperately searching for any sign of a person outside.

He almost had a heart attack as his own face suddenly appeared on the other side of the window. This Third Todd started turning the handle on the outside of the door. He pounded on the window and pointed down for First Todd to do the same. Todd got up and they tried turning it together.

Finally, it began to move.

Once the door was open, Third Todd grabbed him. "I can't explain everything right now, you'll just have to trust me. I've been doing this a while, and I think I have it figured out."

He reached into his pocket and pulled out a cell phone battery. "Where's the phone?"

First Todd glanced back at the bits of plastic and circuitry on the floor of the time machine. He slowly pointed at it.

"Damn. Why do we always do that?" Third Todd paced back and forth. "Okay, how about the key card?"

"No, but it has to be in here somewhere."

"Actually, it won't be, because you haven't lost it yet. But don't worry, I have a few extras."

~*~

The identical men were discussing how they were going

to proceed when they heard a strange humming noise that Third Todd recognized as the time machine in action.

When Fourth Todd appeared, they explained the situation to him. He was confused about one thing, though. "How come all of us aren't appearing at the exact same time?"

First Todd didn't have a clue, but Third Todd had it figured it out. "Every time it happens, events are slightly different. The scientist dude didn't have time to be exact, so the tiniest difference causes us to go back to different points in the past."

"When the hell did we get so smart?"

"I didn't do it on my own. There were other Todds who have been around even longer trying to figure this whole thing out."

The other two Todds answered simultaneously. "*Were?*"

Third Todd shook his head. "You don't wanna know."

Fourth Todd spoke up. "Maybe we do."

Third Todd sighed and led his twins down a long row of machinery and artifacts until he got to a giant freezer in back. He swiped the key card and opened the door.

When the frozen vapor cloud dispersed, they could see dozens of dead Todds, some in relatively decent shape, others missing body parts or completely torn to shreds.

First Todd was nervous now. "Exactly how many times have we tried this kind of thing?"

"I don't know. But it's a lot, and most of us don't make it through. Every time we seem to have it down, something goes wrong. We've tried calling ourselves at various points, stopping ourselves from coming in here in different ways, escaping from this facility...and half the time it's another one of us who messes everything up. But I think I've finally figured out a way that will work."

Third Todd shut the door. "Here's the plan…"

~*~

First Todd stayed hidden around the corner as the scientist and the guards arrived at the security door where Second Todd had just gone through, and the guards finally got the door open. Since he had failed to stop the new him from entering the room, the plan was shot—he'd have to improvise.

Just as the guards got the door open and went through, Todd jumped out of hiding and grabbed the scientist by the back of his lab coat. He threw him down and sat on the small man's chest.

The scientist's eyes went wide. "Wha—I thought—"

Todd covered his mouth. "Stop talking. If you don't do what I say, you're dead."

It seemed like an eternity before the monster was loose and the shots and screaming began. Todd took his hand off the scientist's mouth. "Hear that? I just saved your life. Now follow me…"

~*~

Todd barely had enough time to explain things to the scientist before they got to the time machine. Since the scientist wasn't there to direct the latest Todd to the machine, the creature would be chasing him around elsewhere in the warehouse.

"Remember, take your time and make sure you send me back far enough. If this works, none of this will have ever happened." Todd opened the door to the time machine and recoiled as he smelled the rotting corpse. To the scientist's dismay, he pulled the corpse from the chamber and left it sitting right in front of the machine. Todd pointed to his dead clone. "And make sure you set it for the door to unlock so I'm not trapped in there again."

Through the small window, Todd could see his other self being torn limb by limb by the creature at the other end of the warehouse. Would there be enough time for the scientist to get the calculations right this time?

The bright light and lurching feeling didn't hit him by surprise this time, but they were just as dramatic and he still passed out.

When Todd awoke, he immediately checked the door and saw that he was able to get out. He checked the guard schedule Third Todd had given him and matched it against the time on the retro-tech console for the time machine. Just right.

He stood next to the door and waited for the guard to arrive on his routine check, heavy object at the ready. When the guy came through, he didn't even have time to register the presence of another person before Todd knocked him out cold. Todd changed into his uniform, which worked despite being a little too big except for around the waist, where it was really snug. Luckily, these guys even wore shades indoors.

Between the uniform and the key card, getting out wasn't much of a problem. In fact, Todd was practically home free before he ran into his only difficulty during his escape—another him. Apparently, this Todd had come up with the same idea of stealing a guard's uniform and didn't realize who he was attacking when he leaped from hiding and knocked First Todd to the ground.

Fifth Todd lifted his fist and was about to hit him again. "Wait, Todd! It's me!"

The newer Todd pulled off the dark glasses and saw his own face. "Jesus, man, what the hell is going on here?"

First Todd tried to summarize the whole thing as fast as possible. Fifth Todd agreed to go along with the plan, and even provide a diversion inside while First Todd was getting out of the compound.

"Just one thing," he said. "What happens to us if your plan works?"

First Todd shrugged. "Dunno. I guess we all disappear. What do you think?"

"Sounds right to me, I guess."

~*~

"Depends on what you want to use it for," said the old man behind the counter.

"Well, I'm gonna be gluing cloth to plastic." Todd was holding up two different types of super glue.

"I'd say they're 'bout the same. Go with the cheaper one."

"Sounds good." Todd paid for the glue and left the store giddy with anticipation for his next practical joke. He read the instructions on the package of the super glue on his way down the alley to the parking lot in back, and realized someone was blocking his way. "'Scuse me."

"Look at me," said a familiar voice.

Todd almost fell back when he saw himself standing in front of him. "Man, you almost gave me a heart attack." He stood up close to the other Todd and looked his face over.

"Dude, that is awesome. Who put you up to this? Is that, like, a professional makeup job, or prosthetics, or what?"

"No. Listen to me…"

"Man, there's no way he found someone that looks *that* much like me. No frikkin' way."

"Todd, I *am* you. I'm from the future."

New Todd burst out laughing. "This is freakin' great! Is there a camera? Am I being punked or something?" He looked around the alley for some sign of recording devices.

The look-alike took hold of him by the front of his shirt. "You have to follow my instructions. *Don't* pull that prank on Jeff, *don't* go looking at ads in the newspaper, and most of all *don't* go volunteering for any experiments for some extra cash."

Todd pulled his twin's hands off his shirt. "Look, I don't know who you think you are, but this is getting out of hand. I'm gonna do what I want, and some goon hired by Jeff isn't gonna scare me off, no matter how much you look like me."

Angry, New Todd stalked down the alley toward his car. Desperate, First Todd picked up a cement block and lifted it high.

New Todd finally realized the gravity of his situation and looked First Todd in the eyes. "Wait...you really are me?"

"Something like that." First Todd slammed the block down and broke it over New Todd's head. He fell like a sack of potatoes and blood streamed from his ears. First Todd checked for a pulse. The other him was dead.

First Todd expected to disappear from reality now that there was no way for this version of himself to exist. He looked at his hands, expecting them to start fading away, but nothing happened.

After making sure nobody was around, First Todd put the other Todd's body into a dumpster full of compost. He made sure it was completely covered and wondered what would happen if the body was found. *Well, if they identify the body as me, I'll just have to show them that they're wrong.*

As he was about to walk away, Todd noticed a bag on the ground and picked it up. He pulled out the super glue and looked it over, and couldn't help smiling at the practical joke he remembered playing even though it would never actually happen now.

He tossed the glue into the dumpster and walked to his car. After all, he didn't want to be late for work.

~*~

Wrench

Paul K. Swardstrom

~*~

WRENCH... ROXANNE BLINKAKED AND SHOOK the cobwebs out of her head. For a moment, she could have sworn she was a clerk in the corner bodega.

"Rox," Dina hissed. "Get it together. Jay Jay is watching." Dina sauntered to the corner, waving to a man with his window down.

Roxanne didn't have any time to think about it as another car pulled up.

"Hey, baby," she crooned to the John in the car.

To her surprise, the guy wasn't even looking at her. He was looking down at some device in his lap and muttering. "This isn't right. No way."

"Baby doll," she interrupted.

The guy looked up at her with an expression of horror. "Whatever's going on, I'm sure I can help you." She swayed suggestively to emphasize the point.

The guy in the car looked horrified. "I'm sorry, Rosie. So sorry. I'll fix it, I will," he said.

Roxanne lost interest and stood up to go looking for another John. Behind her, she heard the man finish, "...right...

now!"

Wrench... Rosalee blinked and leaned over to the microphone. "Now serving number one-oh-eight at window twelve." She yawned and let her thoughts drift to thoughts of Salisbury Steak and Gilmore Girls before the next client stepped up to the window.

Before the old woman could reach the counter, a disheveled man barged in ahead of her. "Excuse me. This is urgent," he explained.

"Sir," Rosalee interjected. "This woman was next in line."

The woman he had pushed aside huffed.

The man vigorously nodded. "Yes, yes. My business is urgent, Rosie. I was told to come to this window when my form was completed." He handed a stack of papers to Rosalee.

She thumbed through them quickly and put the other woman back in the queue. She entered information into her terminal while the man turned his attention to a device in his hand.

"Is that your phone?" she asked. It was rather blocky. It didn't look quite look like a phone.

"No. It's my remote control," he murmured.

Her eyelids lifted slightly. "Remote? For what?"

"I'm going to fix this, Rosie," he said, ignoring her question.

Rosalee stopped what she was doing and stared at him. "My name is Rosalee. What are you going to fix?"

Wrench... Rosalee... no, Rosette teetered in the hallway while teenagers bumped for position as they rushed or sauntered to class.

"Are you okay, Miss Oaks?" a passing student asked.

Was she? It felt like vertigo. "I'll be okay, Sammy. Thanks." She walked a bit further and ducked into the teacher's lounge, then grabbed a bottle of water.

Sitting on the couch, she placed her head between her knees. In a moment, Rosette heard a shuffle, then footsteps coming toward her. She peeked up when the feet appeared in front of her. It was a slightly disheveled man wearing a substitute badge.

"Are you okay?" he asked.

"Just a bit of vertigo," she answered.

"Hmmm... perhaps some smaller skips," he said to himself.

"What?" Rosette jerked her head up. The man was fiddling with a blocky device.

"I messed up, Rosie. It was bad. You should have seen yourself..." he seemed to notice her watching and paused.

"Who are you?"

"Gordon, my dear." His attention was back on the device in his hands.

Rosette covered the device. "Tell me more," she implored.

His eyes looked into hers, and she could see the trembling at the corners. Whoever he was, he was a torn and desperate man.

"We invented a time machine, you and me. We went back in time before you were born and... something changed when we came back. I've been trying to fix it ever since."

The man looked as if he hadn't slept in days. Rosette didn't know him, but her heart went out to him.

He looked at the thing. "I think your vertigo is likely related to the kind of jumps I'm making. We made a mess in the past. I'm trying to put it all back together again, but..."

"Hey," she started. "You know, maybe you just need to..."

Wrench...

Rosalind taped the package across the top. "That'll be $7.95 to ship to Vegas."

Wrench...

Roshenna turned the final card over. "Dealer gets a ten. Dealer wins."

Wrench...

Rosita tucked the flower in her hair.

Wrench...

Rosenda placed the bill on the president's desk. "Madame, these are ready for you to sign."

Wrench...

Roslyn Ochs signed with a flourish and posed for a picture at her oval office desk.

Wrench...

Roz could see the suspect in the speeding car ahead. "All agents converge on agent Oaches," she heard in her ear.

Wrench...

Rosinda slammed on the brakes as the agency cars sped past. She glanced at the meter. At least she'd get a little bit more out of the fare.

Wrench ...

Rosa Anne flipped the ratchet handle in her hand before applying it to the engine bolt above her head. Someone had been driving this taxi a little too rough.

She heard the side door open, and then an oddly familiar shuffle. She had a sinking feeling, but couldn't say why. She grabbed her 15/16 and slid herself out from under the car.

"Can I help ya?" she asked to the open air.

A man in a disheveled suit turned around. He was looking down at a device. "We're getting close, Rosie. One or two more."

Rosa Anne clocked him with her wrench. The device clattered down and the man hit the floor a second later. He didn't even see it coming.

She stared quizzically at the wrench for a moment, wondering why she had just done that to this man she didn't even know. She bent over him and checked.

He was still breathing.

Rosa Anne breathed a sigh of relief. That was good. She picked up the device.

Wrench.

~*~

Gramps

Ernie Howard

~*~

IT WAS AMAZING to Tate that, on such a beautiful day, someone he knew was dying. *How could anyone or anything die on a day like this?* The trees he walked under were full with green leaves and buzzed with energy, full of life. The leaves' colors were accented by amber rays of sunlight that gave life. Cars rolled down the street with occupants who gazed out of windows and passed a smile with Tate. Everyone and everything was alive. But only a few feet away from all this life, an old man lay in a bed. His ninety-seven years were experiencing their last hours on this earth.

Tate's Aunt Macy had called him yesterday and told him his grandpa was close, and that Gramps had been asking for Tate, which was odd. Not because he and his grandfather disliked each other, but because they hadn't talked to each other for about three years. Gramps was in his nineties, and Tate was young and lived what might as well have been a world away on the west coast. Their lives were very different, and they didn't have much to talk about.

Tate had walked the mile from the airport to his grandfather's house. He always traveled light no matter where he went. So, the walk with just his backpack was enjoyable. He stopped in front of the house and stared up at it. The place looked small, but it had been a long time since Tate had seen it.

When you're a kid, everything looks big.

The place needed a coat of paint. He couldn't get himself to go in just yet. *What do you say to a dying man?* Tate sat on the front steps, watching life play out before him, and lost track of time.

"Tate! When did you get here, Hun?"

Tate spun around and looked up at his Aunt Macy. He couldn't keep the smile off his face. His aunt was one of those people who could be slightly overweight but still exude health and beauty. She looked down at Tate with blue eyes that hadn't lost any luster over the years. Aunt Macy was still an attractive lady, even though she was in her sixties with only one wrinkle on her face except for a slight crinkle around her eyes.

"Hey, Aunt Macy," Tate said.

He stood up and barely had his footing before his aunt grabbed him by the shoulders and planted a huge smooch on his cheek. Aunt Macy pushed Tate back a foot and looked at him. Her eyes could always find the truth. The lady had a sixth sense. Tate had only tried to lie to his aunt once, and never again.

"He just wants to see you, Tate. You were always his favorite," Aunt Macy said.

Tate nodded and averted his eyes, not wanting Aunt Macy to read him. "I know, Macy."

"Go inside. He's in his room. You still know where it is, right?"

Tate nodded his head yes. It was funny. You could move two thousand miles away. You could have a career where a lot of people depended on you and make more money than you ever thought you would. You were an adult. Doing adult things. But the minute your aunt puts her hand on your back, giving you a nudge to go see your grandpa, you instantly turn into a little kid again.

The house smelled old but not unpleasant. The air had a

lingering scent of some sort of lemon scented disinfectant. It reminded Tate of being a kid once again. He looked down at the floor. The old rug that he'd raced his Hotwheels on numerous times looked like it had been cleaned recently. Tate was not surprised by its upkeep and the general neatness of the house. Aunt Macy didn't mess around when it came to housework.

The hallway to the right that lead to the bedrooms was dark. Tate looked down it and saw a ghostly white light reflecting off the wall at the end of the hallway, compliments of a muted television. Gramps always fell asleep with a TV on but with no sound. Tate had never understood it.

He followed the light, glancing at the walls as he passed. Pictures of goofy, smiling kids and parents who were happy with each other for at least one day hung on the walls.

His grandfather lay in bed with his mouth open. If Tate hadn't seen the slow rise of the man's chest, he would have thought Gramps had already passed. Tate waked into the room and cleared his throat, hoping to rouse his grandpa.

"I'm not asleep, boy. Just resting my eyes," Gramps said.

Gramps had said this since Tate was little. It was like his grandpa thought taking naps were a sign of weakness.

"I didn't think you were, Gramps, just had a catch in my throat," Tate said. He was trying to hide the mischievous smile that was threatening to show itself.

"Ya, sure. And I'm a springy young boy, prancing through a meadow of flowers," Gramps said.

Same old Gramps. The man was on death's door and still the sarcasm flowed out of his mouth like honey on a warm summer day. "How are you feeling, Gramps?"

"You know, that's the problem with your generation. Always wanting to know how everyone feels. Well, Tate my boy." Gramps paused, and smiled a mischievous smile that looked very similar to Tate's a moment ago. "I feel like shit. I happen to be dying." Gramps let out with a raspy laugh that turned into a coughing fit. Tate looked around for a Kleenex or a cloth but couldn't find one in the vicinity. Gramps was shooing him away with his left hand, and wiping his mouth with his sheet with his right hand. Tate sat back into his chair and waited for his grandpa to settle before he started up the conversation again.

"You know what I meant, Gramps," Tate said.

Gramps put his hand up to stop him. "I know Tate, just giving you some grief. Enough with the pleasantries, son. Let's get to the point, why I wanted to see you before I die."

Tate looked at his grandpa's wrinkled face. The general facial features said old, but Gramps' eyes danced and were full of fire that his own had never held. The man had something important to say. "I'm here Gramps." He reached out for his Grandpa's hand. Gramps grabbed Tate's hand and squeezed. He was surprised at the strength his Grandfather still possessed. The old man sighed and patted Tate's hand, his smile leaving.

I need you to believe everything I am about to say. It's not going to be a long spiel, just a declaration and some instructions. All I ask is that you believe it, because I have never lied to you. Can you do that for me?"

Gramps' eyes had become even more fierce. Tate had always done what his grandfather told him. There were many dead weeds that could attests to that. But something about the way his grandfather was speaking had the feel of the onset of dementia. Gramps had never asked Tate to believe him. Tate just did. "I'll believe it, Gramps. Just spit it out."

"You saved my life," Gramps said.

Tate had been holding his breath and he let it out, feeling relief wash over him. Gramps wasn't losing it, he was finding his feelings. Finding a higher power. "I love you too, Gramps."

Gramps rolled his eyes. "I don't mean metaphorically, dummy. I mean for real. You saved my ass during the war." The old man's face was serious. One bushy eyebrow was raised, telling Tate to take it or leave it.

Tate squeezed his grandfather's hand and looked at him with pity. "I don't understand what you mean, Gramps." Tate knew he was breaking the rules. Everything he had heard about dementia said you were supposed to go along with what the person was saying, but Tate couldn't let himself go along with it.

Gramps rolled his eyes again. Tate had only seen his grandpa mad once, and his anger wasn't over something small like not believing what the man had said. Tate didn't want to upset his grandpa, so he decided from here on out he would just go along with whatever the old man told him. "I'm sorry. I believe you, but I just don't understand what you're getting at." Tate was trying to keep his expressions neutral.

"I know how this sounds to you. I don't have dementia. This is the truth. I have been holding this secret in me for over seventy years." Gramps eyes looked lonely and defeated. "Can you imagine what that was like?" Gramps looked at Tate. The old man's eyes searched for answers. "I told your grandmother once. When we were young." Gramps looked away. Tate could almost see the years on the man's face. Gramps snorted a short laugh. "She thought I was loony toons too. But just as I told your grandma long ago, you can think me crazy but the truth is the truth."

"I don't think you're crazy, Gramps. But I do think dying is stressful." Tate said. He smiled, trying to keep things light.

"Oh, hell with it. Time is running short and I would suspect we have had this conversation many times. Best to just get on with it. You do it in the attic. The box is up there, opened already," Gramps said.

"What do I do in the attic?" Tate was looking at his grandfather with general concern.

Gramps raised his eyebrows and looked at Tate like he had never met anyone dumber. "Have you not been paying attention? You travel back in time and save my life Tate."

He was trying not to show concern, it would only make his grandfather more upset. He was going with it. "Okay, okay."

"You had better wipe that look off your face and get your attitude right. Because your life… Scratch that. Your existence and my short life at the time depend on it." Gramps sat back. The old man's breathing had become raspy. Tate could hear a low wheeze with every one of his grandfather's breaths.

"Okay. What do I need to do?" He needed to calm the man down. He would play along even if the man told him to dress up in a dress and walk down the street.

"I put the box up in the attic when you were ten years old. You were out playing in the front yard with your sister, and you turned and looked at me. The features of your face had finally caught up with the memory of the man I had seen long ago. I saw who you were. Who you would become. So, I got things ready, just like you told me to do. The box and its contents have been laying directly in the middle of the attic floor for twenty years," Gramps said. He rubbed his forehead and sighed. "I'm tired, and my body hurts. I have done my part. I have lived in this old shell until the right time. My work is done. Now it's your turn to pull the cart some."

Tate didn't know what to say. Of course, he would do what Gramps had asked of him. "When do I need to do this?" Tate said.

Gramps looked at Tate and raised his brows once again.

"Oh. Okay, Gramps. I'll get started," Tate said. He patted his grandfather's hand and let go, grunting as he got up from the chair. Tate turned to leave the room. Gramps stopped him before he could.

"Tate. This is very important. Follow the instructions. Don't be scared. There were no bullets on that day," Gramps said.

Tate nodded his head and tried to match the old man's expression. "I will Gramps."

The old man closed his eyes, ignoring the blue haze of the TV. Tate looked one more time at his grandpa, and left silently.

~*~

Tate could hear his aunt talking to someone on the porch. He stood in the living room, not sure of what to do next. The conversation was one-sided, so he figured she was on the phone. He crossed the living room, hoping she didn't see him. He was going to do what Gramps had asked him to do. He didn't want to have to explain himself to his aunt. The poor lady would think he'd lost it just like Gramps.

The stairs to the attic sat at the back of the house. When Tate was a kid, they'd scared the hell out of him. They were the skinny stairs that went up to the darkness. Now they just looked old and unused. He walked to the first step and the old wood creaked under his foot. He wondered when was the last time anyone had used these stairs.

He got to the top of the stairs and opened the door that lead into the attic. The light shined brightly through the large window at the other end of the room. He winced until his eyes could properly adjust to the sunlight. Tate walked through the door and closed it behind him.

The attic looked exactly like it had twenty years ago. Every box and piece of furniture was in the same place and coated with a fine layer of dust. His old tricycle sat in one corner. Rust had finally overtaken the red paint, making the metal look orange instead of the original red.

Tate spotted footprints on the wood floor. They were old. The dust they were made in were covered with another layer of dust. He followed them and ended up directly in the middle of the room were a small cigar box sat. He wasted no time and walked to the box. He bent down and opened the box's top flap, and eyed the two pieces inside. An old wristwatch that, judging by the still second hand, hadn't been telling time for a while, and a piece of paper that was folded up into a tight and neat square.

Tate picked up the letter carefully. The paper felt old and brittle in his hands. He was careful as he pulled back the folds to reveal the writing on the inside.

The letter was dated June 8th, 1944.

It was short only a paragraph long.

Instructions

Hold the watch between your thumb and forefinger. Wait thirty seconds. Come and save my life, Tate. I just met you an hour ago. I am already so proud of you, son.

He reread the short paragraph a couple times. "That's it?" he said to the room. His head swam. *How is any of this possible?* Gramps was always good at pulling pranks, but there was something about the letter and the wristwatch that felt real. The objects gave him the creeps. Curiosity and a sense of duty won over the creepy feeling and Tate picked up the wristwatch. Holding it with his thumb and pointer finger. He looked around the room. If anyone had been there, he would have felt stupid. He felt a little dumb and he was alone.

Tate was about to put the watch back and forget all about this when the old attic turned to a blue sky and a muddy dirt road. He could hear marching boots and machinery. He spun on his heel and bumped into a marching soldier.

"Hey! Where in the hell did you come from?"

Tate was staring into the eyes of a much younger version of his grandfather. His words felt thick and clumsy on his tongue. "You're, you're, you're young," Tate said.

"All right, there. Take it easy." His grandfather put his hand on his shoulder and steadied him.

Tate shook off his surprise quick. If he was in 1944, that meant he had to save his grandfather's life. The time was now. Any minute something bad was going to happen.

The jeep came out of nowhere. Gramps would have never seen it coming or heard it over the loud tanks and other vehicles. Tate grabbed his grandfather by his jacket and pulled him backwards into the mud just as the jeep barreled down on them. It was gone in less than a second. Tate was feeling good about himself until he heard his grandfather scream out in pain. The word *existence* flashed in his mind as he searched his Gramps for any wounds. Tate looked down and saw his leg pointed at an odd angle. *The old man had always told me his limp was from a motorcycle accident,* Tate thought. Now he knew better.

Gramps, being the tough guy, stifled his scream and held his crooked leg. Tate could see a soldier running up the line of marching men, the familiar red cross of a medic on his helmet.

"That guy came out of nowhere," the medic said. The man crouched in front of Gramps and looked at his legs. He whistled between his teeth. "This is a bad one. Looks like you just got a ticket to a warm bed and hot meals, private."

Gramps nodded his head and grimaced with pain. "I would have been toast if it hadn't been for this guy," Gramps said. He pointed up at Tate standing over him.

The medic gave Tate a once over, and made a face like he had smelled something bad. "Right... Let me see if I can get you a stretcher. Sit tight." The medic made the motion of patting Gramps' leg and thought better of it. He got up and jogged back the way he had come.

Tate took the opportunity to give Gramps the instructions and the watch. He talked rapidly, knowing his grandpa understood everything he was saying. When he finished telling all that he knew, he stood back up and looked down at the young version of Gramps. A kid who looked up in confusion, but with a fierceness in his eyes. This kid would become his grandfather. Tate held out the watch. Gramps looked at it and moved his hand towards it and grabbed it. Tate let go.

A dust mote floated past his eyes, catching a ray of sun just in time to make it look like a golden snowflake. He was back in the attic. A wave of nausea threatened, but Tate managed to hold in his food. He got up on legs that felt surprisingly strong.

The memory of his young Grandpa was fading.

"What an odd dream," he said to the empty room.

"Tate." Aunt Macy stood in the doorway of the attic. "He's gone, Tate. Gramps has passed." Aunt Macy wiped a tear from her cheek.

Tate wanted to laugh at the irony. In his dream, he had saved his grandpa from death, and now he was dead. He looked at Aunt Macy, feeling oddly relived. He walked over to her and put his arms around her. They stayed like that for a while, and then Aunt Macy pulled away.

"Tate. Where did all this mud come from?" Aunt Macy said.

The woman had mud on her hands. Dark mud. Tate looked down at his boots, and saw he had tracked mud across the attic floor. The dizziness came back strong. He saw the world go dark. His last thought was he had been there. In France. In 1944.

~*~

Lorem Tempus
Daniel Arthur Smith

~*~

THE SOFT RESONATION OF THE MEDITATION GONG accompanied Renton on his solemn march toward death. Whether death waited or not, every journey to the chambers was treated with the same reverence. A hooded cowl hid his head. His arms were crossed and lost in draping sleeves of his long white robe. Everything here was white, his robe, the corridor, and the interior of the ziggurat above—white to eliminate distraction. In the academy, he learned that white represented the Bureau's neutrality in the spectrum. His tenure in the Bureau taught him otherwise. The protocol required a clear mind.

Breathing in and out with the gong, he gently trod until he reached the glass door of the chamber. When the door slid silently to the side, he entered. The room was no bigger than a light ship confessional or the shrines used by those still worshipping the ancients and—with the bowl and pillow on the floor and the small shelf holding the eyedropper and vision disc—could easily be confused as such. This was fitting. Renton's team was in service to the Bureau rather than any god, yet they were as stalwart in the protocol of discipline and execution as any monastic order.

His task was a simple act, but mind-bending in nature. Unlike other Agents, members of his secret elite order had few if any implants. The protocol was too risky for permanent diatomic nanites and vision was best unsullied by the influence of the ocular upgrades.

Renton sat on the pillow, legs crossed, and prepared himself. The ritual was based on the spiritual path of the Kalachakra, and he could easily ascend without chemical induction, but the protocols were for his safety. The DMT nanite elixir in the drops was meant to be a short lived surgical trip, from which he would secure his next directive.

Back straight, he drew his breaths deeper—in through his nose to a count of four, out through his mouth to a count of five—in rhythm to the meditation gong. As he repeated the breaths, moments passed, his heart slowed. The base of his spine grew warm, the root chakra. He focused only on the counting and let all other thoughts fall away—in, one, two, three, four—out, one, two, three, four, five. The heat from his tail bone spread into his belly. A euphoric rolling ball of fire scorching his gut as it spread. This was the sacral chakra, the gateway to connection. With the warmth came the desire to pull the meditation inward. But he did not go inward, he went the way of the protocol. It had taken years of discipline to achieve this balance.

Renton continued his breathing, letting the energy manifest from his belly up to his stomach then into his chest. With each breath, the energy flowed further out into his arms until his fingers tingled.

On his next exhale, in rhythm to the count, he reached for the dropper, slowly whispering, "I take the drops, for this I cannot change."

He drew the dropper close to his heart.

"I accept I'll fear, but this I cannot change."

He tilted his head back.

"I accept my past, for this I cannot change."

He raised the dropper.

"I accept my future, for this I cannot change."

He dripped three drops into his left eye.

"I accept my path, for this I cannot change."

He let three drops fall to his right eye.

"I accept my directive, for this I cannot change."

Then, eyes wide open, he straightened his head and gazed into the pearl white disc before him.

"I accept I'll fear, but this I cannot change."

DMT coursed through his brain, triggering the nanites to a series of diatomic flops. The warmth within him boiled and, with a jolt, an electric quiver shot up his spine.

Renton's throat compressed, his breathing stopped, and the flesh of his face pulled tight as the chamber ripped away from around him. Only the vision disc remained, its pearl white face a swirling kaleidoscope of misting grays.

The grays fragmented into wisps of color, then stabilized to an image at the center of the swirl.

Pictured was a large indoor space, but with trees and foliage, perhaps a garden arcade. Everything was tinted in blue, and there was music. The faint notes of a saxophone. Renton tensed to keep focus, to fight the full body euphoria. The image held. People, in gowns and suits—no, *tuxedoes*—grouped in front of exhibitions—no, *statues*—a sculpture garden lit by blue neon. Still not enough information. Aiming the view point was dangerous, could close the mind bridge. He had to trust. Then, at once, the point of view shifted to more people, seated at round white clothed tables. To the side, beneath a willow, the jazz trio. Then someone who shouldn't be there.

The vision delivered his directive.

A wave of nausea, tentacles lashing in his peripheral, and the vision was gone.

The chamber returned.

A turbulent rush of nausea forced him to convulse, to constrict forward. He grabbed for the bowl to his side and hurled and heaved and gagged. Nothing left him.

The cramps calmed but his body quivered in a rapid chill. A drop of sweat trickled from his hairline into his eye. He blinked the burning away then wiped his eyes with the back of his wet hand.

Renton tried to stand, but collapsed back to the pillow under his own weight. He succeeded in his second attempt by leaning on the wall.

"Let me help you." Renton recognized the voice from behind. It was Director Lin.

Renton faced the handsome Korean. The muscles in his throat were still tight. He let a stretched silence hang between them while he swallowed, then, when the gong resonated again, extended his hand. "Yes," he said, then forced the words, "That would be good."

The Director—out of place in his indigo silk suit—smiled and gently took hold of Renton's upper arm. Renton marveled at the blue of the Director's ocular implants, and the smoothness of his eternally youthful nanite preserved skin. It was hard for Renton to believe the young Director was easily a century older than him.

"Are you okay?" the Director asked.

"You'd think I'd be used to this," said Renton. He let the Director guide him to the corridor. "It will pass."

"I can request a med shot for you. Relax you a bit."

"I don't mend with the help of nanites."

"But you're obviously not yourself. I'm sure the order would allow the exception, if I secured the shot."

"Abstinence is not a requirement. It's a personal choice. Without the reparation of the nanites, the vision maintains its clarity, remains in the forefront of my mind."

Renton stumbled toward the corridor wall. Director Lin threw his arm around Renton's waist.

"I'm okay," said Renton.

"You know," said the Director, "there are only so many times you can perform the protocol. You're near the limit."

"I have no worry of that. After a nap, I'll be myself."

"And what about the next time?"

"The directive was clear. There will be no next time."

"So it's true."

"Yes. In two days, at the Winthrop, there is a gala in the Upper garden atriums overlooking the city. There will be an infiltrator. I will be waiting for him."

"What else did you see?"

"You already know. The gala is to pay tribute to you. Loudon is there. As your liaison, I'm sure he briefed you."

"He did. You will be successful in stopping the incursion. But, as a result—"

"As a result, I will die."

"No."

"But I saw my future, and my future cannot be changed."

"You saw your future. But you did not see your end."

"So that's what brings the director down to the restricted levels? You're here to tell me face to face that the fall does not kill me? That I become a vegetable?"

"On the contrary. I'm here to tell you that you'll be promoted."

"That's kind. But I have no heirs to receive the additional benefit."

"I told you. You're not going to die. Not as you may expect anyway."

"I'm not going to let you resuscitate me in a cyber shell. I won't approve. My 'end of life' statement is clear—no extreme measures."

They had reached a crossroads in their conversation and the underground level. In the intersection was a small fountain pool and a bench.

"Let's sit," said the Director. He helped Renton ease down, sat next to him, removed a flask from his jacket, then handed it to the exhausted man.

Renton lifted his hand. "No," he said. "I can't. Not yet."

"Oh. It's not alcohol. It's water. The filtration systems dry out the lower levels. I'm easily parched."

Renton accepted and drew from the flask.

"I want to assure you," the Director continued. "We will not be modifying you in any way."

"Good then. I guess." The gong chimed.

"We won't need to."

"What does that mean?"

"Do you remember when Lucian left the order?"

"Left? He was killed on his last directive."

"He wasn't."

"Of course, he was. He was my mentor. I read the eulogy." Renton took another drink of the warm water. "You were there."

"It was a nice service. A memorial."

"There was no body. He was vaporized in the explosion."

"What if I told you he wasn't? That he got away?"

"You mean he quanted? Jumped to another spectral plane?"

"Not exactly. He jumped time."

"I assure you. That's not how it works. What we see in the meditation chamber is simply a chemically induced déjà vu. If we were to actually cross the mind bridge, to travel, we'd only be able to move back and forth through the cycle of our lives. It's a path to madness. That's why the protocol is so tight, so that we may only glimpse our future."

"You see your directive and the path to achieve it. Do you really think your mentor, a master of martial arts and weaponry, simply failed? After countless successful directives?"

"We only glimpse our future. We cannot change it."

"Let me ask you. Was it because you glimpsed the future that led to your success in each directive? You knew to wait in the hangar for Goretz, and that he was going to draw a sabre on you. You knew that the terrorists at the plaza were going to where suicide belts. How is that you, a Tempus Agent, fall from the Gardens?"

"You see, that's the kind of thinking that leads to madness. Did I choose the number because I knew I'd choose the number? It's simple. I have to fall. I have no choice. The future—"

"The future cannot be changed. You're right. All I'm telling you is that you're supposed to fall."

"I just said that," smirked Renton. His strength was

returning.

"This is something different. These men will take you to rest, to prepare you for your indoctrination."

Renton raised his head. A cloaked figure approached, with a uniformed medic on either side.

"Indoctrination?"

"As you're aware, the Tempus are secret to even the highest levels of the Bureau. But there is yet an even higher level of ascension. The Lorem Tempus."

"An Elite Temporal Agent? A true time traveler? That's a myth."

"No," said the cloaked figure. "It's an ascended state of being."

The timber of the voice was all too familiar to Renton. "It can't be," he said. "Lucien?"

The cloaked man pulled his cowled hood back to reveal his face. "Yes," he said. "It's me. The gala is in two days. You will rest, and then you will be taught what you need to know."

"What I need to know?"

"How to quant to a temporal plane," said Lucian. "From there you'll be able to move beyond this point in the time cycle."

"Quant? I don't wish to be modified."

"You already are. The doses, you don't need them anymore. In fact, they've compounded. You have amazing skills that are about to be unleashed."

"Why now?"

The Director placed his hand on Renton's shoulder. "Because you're ready, and because you're needed."

"There is a rogue agent," said Lucien. "I need your help in dealing with him. His actions have rippled."

"That's ridiculous," said Renton. "We can't change the past or future."

"He hasn't changed anything. He's already done what he's going to do. As have we."

"As have we?" asked Renton.

"When you pull the infiltrator through the hole in the

atrium wall," said Lucien, "you'll experience a spectral shift."

"It will be then," said Director Lin. "That you'll become a true time traveler. A Lorem Tempus."

~*~

ABOUT THE AUTHORS

Nathan M. Beauchamp started writing stories at nine years old and never stopped. From his first grisly tales about carnivorous catfish, mole detectives, and cyborg housecats, his interests have always delved into strange waters. Nathan works in finance so that he can support his habit of putting words together in the hope that someone will read them. His hobbies include reading, photography, arguing for sport, and pondering the eventual heat death of the universe. He has published many short stories in magazines and anthologies, and holds an MFA in creative writing from Western State. He lives in Colorado with his wife and two young boys. Nathan co-created the award winning YA science fiction series **Universe Eventual** where he writes as N.J. Tanger. The series includes *Chimera*, *Helios*, and *Ceres* and the prequel *Ascension*. **Universe Eventual**.

For more information, visit njtanger.com

Paul K. Swardstrom is a husband and a father, a music teacher by day and family man at night. I write when I can and am enjoying the ride.
A Sun Devil who grew up all over but remembers Michigan fondly, I have settled in Oregon.

Christopher J. Valin is a writer, teacher, artist, and historian living in the Los Angeles area. He received his masters' degree with honors in military history from American Military University and his bachelor's degree in history from the University of Colorado-Colorado Springs. Christopher is the 5x-great-grandson of Sir Charles Douglas, the subject of his book, Fortune's Favorite: Sir Charles and the Breaking of the Line.

In addition to writing and inking for independent comic book companies and writing screenplays for production companies, Christopher has had numerous short stories published in anthologies such as *Clockwork & Capes: Superheroes in the Age of Steam* and *Doomed: Tales of the Last Days*. His screenplays, teleplays, and stories have won several awards and contests.

For more information, visit christophervalin.com

Ernie Howard was born on January 29, 1977 during a Minnesota blizzard. His two story telling parents almost didn't make it to the hospital in their beat up blue Cadillac. Ernie is the writer of *Write Something!*, a book about the illusion of Writers Block. *A World Without*, a Science Fiction book about the love between a husband and wife, and the darkness that can come into a marriage. *Walter*, A Science Fiction book about a boy who is an outcast who makes a friend with a man that speaks to him through his television. Ernie lives with his wife and 3 boys in Henderson, NV, where he dreams up new stories, and tries to live everyday to the fullest.

Daniel Arthur Smith is the author of the international bestsellers *Hugh Howey Lives*, *The Cathari Treasure*, *The Somali Deception*, and a few other novels and short stories. He also curates the phenomenal short fiction series *Tales from the Canyons of the Damned*.

He was raised in Michigan and graduated from Western Michigan University where he studied philosophy, with focus on cognitive science, meta-physics, and comparative religion. He began his career as a bartender, barista, poetry house proprietor, teacher, and then became a technologist and futurist for the Fortune 100 across the Americas and Europe.

Daniel has traveled to over 300 cities in 22 countries, residing in Los Angeles, Kalamazoo, Prague, Crete, and now writes in Manhattan where he lives with his wife and young sons.

For more information, visit danielarthursmith.com

~*~